D0520346

Monster Manners

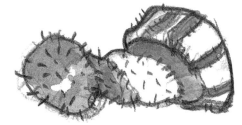

by BETHANY ROBERTS
illustrated by ANDREW GLASS

Clarion Books • New York

Clarion Books
a Houghton Mifflin Company imprint
215 Park Avenue South, New York, NY 10003
Text copyright © 1996 by Barbara Beverage
Illustrations copyright © 1996 by Andrew Glass

The illustrations for this book were executed in watercolor on cold press paper.
The text is set in 18/24-point Kabel medium.

All rights reserved.

For information about permission to reproduce selections from this book,
write to Permissions, Houghton Mifflin Company,
215 Park Avenue South, New York, NY 10003.
For information about this and other Houghton Mifflin
trade and reference books and multimedia products,
visit The Bookstore at Houghton Mifflin on the World Wide Web
at (http://www.hmco.com/trade/).

Printed in the USA

Library of Congress Cataloging-in-Publication Data

Roberts, Bethany.
Monster manners : a guide to monster etiquette / by Bethany Roberts ; illustrated by Andrew Glass.
p. cm.
Summary: An assortment of monsters demonstrates good and bad manners.
ISBN 0-395-69850-2
[1. Monsters—Fiction. 2. Etiquette—Fiction. 3. Stories in rhyme.] I. Glass, Andrew, ill. II. Title.
PZ8.3.R5295Mo 1996
[E]—dc20   94-23219
CIP
AC

WOZ 10 9 8 7 6 5 4 3 2

To Pat,
and all the laughs we've shared.
—B.R.

To Anne,
who guides the hand of Saint Jude with her computer.
—A.G.

"Monsters have no manners," it is said, but it's not true.
Do monsters know their manners?
Sometimes they *don't*, sometimes they *do*.

They might forget their manners
when they cough and sneeze and blow.

But they *sometimes* say "Excuse me,"
and pass tissues to and fro.

Sometimes monsters borrow
and forget to give things back.

But *sometimes* they return things,
with an *extra* little snack.

They might be very messy,
and leave things where they drop.

But they *sometimes* clean their rooms,
and dust and scrub and mop.

Often they're so noisy,
it would give a ghost a scare.

Sometimes they're so quiet
you'd never know they're there.

Monsters yell and quarrel,
and pull each other's hair.

Sometimes they get along just fine,
cooperate and share.

Sometimes they put their toys away,
and even make repairs.

They throw their food and gobble,

and grab and snatch and tease.

But *sometimes* they remember,
and politely pass the peas.

Monsters can be lazy,
and yawn and scowl and pout.

But *sometimes* they are helpful,
and take the garbage out.

Sometimes they're poor losers,
if they don't catch a ball.

And *sometimes* they're good sports,
with cheers and claps for all.

They can be very dirty,
caked with goop a slimy green.

But they *sometimes* take a bath,

until they're squeaky clean.

Monsters push and pull and pinch,

and shout and shove and tug.

But they *sometimes* stop their fighting
to have a triple hug.

Monsters, so you see, have been misunderstood.
Sometimes they are naughty—

but monsters *can* be good!